# HEDGEHOG *for* BREAKFAST

by ANN TURNER

illustrated by LISA McCUE

Macmillan Publishing Company    New York

For Judy P.,
*with love*
—A.T.


To Grandma
*You're always in my heart.*
—L.M.

*Macmillan Publishing Company*
*866 Third Avenue, New York, NY 10022*
*Collier Macmillan Canada, Inc.*
*Printed and bound in Singapore*
*First American Edition*

*10   9   8   7   6   5   4   3   2   1*

*The text of this book is set in 16 point Berkeley Old Style Book.*
*The illustrations are rendered in watercolor, acrylic, and colored pencil on bristol.*

*Library of Congress Cataloging-in-Publication Data*
*Turner, Ann Warren.*
*Hedgehog for breakfast/by Ann Turner;*
*illustrated by Lisa McCue.*
*—1st American ed.     p.     cm.*
*Summary: Papa's statement that he would like to have*
*Mrs. Hedgehog for breakfast leads George and Charles to*
*try to cook her in their kitchen, but their guest does not*
*seem to realize that they intend her for the main course.*
*ISBN 0-02-789241-7*
*[1. Hedgehogs—Fiction.] I. McCue, Lisa, ill. II. Title.*
*PZ7.T8535Hd 1989     [E]—dc19     88-8228  CIP  AC*

"I'd like to have Mrs. Hedgehog for breakfast," Papa
said. "I've never had a hedgehog for breakfast
before. Go and invite her to come to our house."

Papa tucked in his big napkin and smiled.

Mama set the table with her best blue dishes
and pink napkins.

George and Charles set off up the lane to Mrs. Hedgehog's house. She lived in a little dirt den in the side of a bank. On top grew wild roses and summer flowers.

"I don't know if I shall like hedgehog for breakfast," Charles said. He peered in through the entrance to her house. It was dark and dirty.

"She eats snails." George shivered. "And bugs and black beetles and things that scurry in the night."

"She won't taste very good," Charles said. "But Papa said he wants hedgehog for breakfast."

"Hello," Charles called down the dark hole. Something scurried inside, and a small hedgehog poked his nose out into the sunlight.

"Go get your mother," George said. "Hurry."

"Yes?" Mrs. Hedgehog was short and stout with prickles all up and down her back. Charles was sure she would not taste good. Or feel very good going down.

"Papa wants you for breakfast," Charles said. "Mama is laying out her best blue dishes with the pink napkins. Please come."

"Oh, dear." Mrs. Hedgehog wiped her paws on her apron. "And I'm busy cleaning. But if your papa says to come, I mustn't refuse."

She set off down the lane with Charles and George. They looked at each other. Should they take her hand? It might hurt.

Should they offer an arm to lean on? That might hurt, too. They decided to do nothing.

They came to Papa's door—a shining green one set into the hill—and opened it. No one was inside. A pot of water boiled on the clean black stove.

"They really *do* want me for breakfast." Mrs. Hedgehog beamed. "Look at how pretty everything is."

She sat down at the table and put her paws on
the blue plate.

Charles looked at George and whispered, "How
do you cook a hedgehog?"

"In a pot," George whispered. He was the older
of the two and always knew what to do.

"Please come over by the stove, Mrs. Hedgehog,"
George said.

Charles brought a stool. "If you'll just step up
here."

"And put your foot in here." George pointed to
the pot. He knew they couldn't lift her in, for she
was far too prickly.

"How kind your papa is. He knows we don't have hot water at our house for baths." Mrs. Hedgehog smiled. She took off her apron and boots, and climbed in.

Charles took a wooden spoon and began to stir.

"Oh, you *are* kind," Mrs. Hedgehog said. "If you'll just scratch a bit more on my back—just there. Ah!" She sighed. "That's the spot!"

She splashed water about her head and face, rubbed under her arms, and bounded out of the pot.

"Just a *little* bit too hot!" She beamed. "But how kind your papa is to offer me a bath." She put on her apron and boots, and sat at the table with her paws on the blue plate.

Charles looked at George. "Now what?"

George led their guest over to the fireplace.
"Mrs. Hedgehog, if you'll just hold on to this spit, I
think you should dry off nicely."

"If you really think so." Slowly she took off her boots and apron again. "On the other hand, I *am* quite wet." She grasped hold of the big iron spit, and Charles began to turn. Round she went.

Water sprayed off of her and doused the fire.

"Oh, what a shame. I've put out your fire!" She climbed down and put on her boots and tied her apron. "But how nice it is to be dry again." She sat at the table and put her paws on the blue plate.

"Perhaps..." George rubbed his forehead. He wasn't quite sure what to do next.

"Perhaps," Charles said, "you're not quite dry, Mrs. Hedgehog. I think I see some drops of wet on your bristles."

"I'm sure you're right." Their guest felt the top of her head. "It *is* a little wet still. But it will soon dry. When is breakfast, and where are your papa and mama?"

"You'd better come into the oven," Charles said, "before you catch your death of cold. Hedgehogs are particularly susceptible to colds."

He took Mrs. Hedgehog's arm, yelled "Ouch!," dropped it, and led her over to the big black oven.

He opened the door, and a warm blast came out. "Just climb in here, if you please," Charles said.

She took off her boots and apron and climbed into the oven. "A *bit* uncomfortable, don't you think? But if you insist." Her voice echoed inside.

Charles slammed the door shut and dusted his paws. "There! Papa should be pleased. That does it!"

Just then Papa and Mama came in the door. "Where is Mrs. Hedgehog?" they asked. "We went to pick flowers for her."

They put two big bunches of flowers on the table.

"Flowers?" George said.

"Not to cook *with* her?" Charles asked.

"Cook? Cook?" Papa said. "Who said anything about cook? Can't you see the pot of oatmeal on the stove? *That's* for our guest!"

Charles ran to the oven and opened the door. Out stepped Mrs. Hedgehog. She steamed gently in the sun.

"Thank you, Charles. It was getting a bit warm in there. I think I am all dry now." She put on her boots and apron, climbed into a chair, and set her paws on the blue plate.

"Your two sons have been most kind," she said to Papa and Mama. "First they gave me a bath. Then they scrubbed my back. Then they twirled me round to get dry. *And* when I wasn't quite, quite dry, they popped me in that warm little room. How thoughtful they are!"

Papa and Mama smiled at George and Charles.

"How nice to see you, Mrs. Hedgehog," Papa said. "As I told my family this morning, I'd like to have Mrs. Hedgehog for breakfast. It's the neighborly thing to do."

"Indeed it is." She beamed at them.

Charles served the oatmeal, George passed the cream, and they let Mrs. Hedgehog do all the talking.